THIS IS THE HOUSE THAT MONSTERS BUILT

By Steve Metzger

Illustrated by Jared Lee

Scholastic Inc.

For Michael Croland
— S.M.

For my grandparents,
Charles and Blanche Fiock
and Glen and Glee Lee
— J.L.

All rights reserved. Published by Scholastic Inc., *Publishers since 1920*. SCHOLASTIC
and associated logos are trademarks and/or registered trademarks of Scholastic Inc.

ISBN 978-0-545-80592-6

10 9 8 7 6 5 4 3 2 1   16 17 18 19 20

Printed in the U.S.A. 40
First printing 2016

Book design by Leslie Mechanic

This is the spooky house that monsters built.

This is the mummy who raised the wall,
Inside the house that monsters built.

This is the spider who started to crawl,
That shocked the mummy who raised the wall,
Inside the house that monsters built.

This is the werewolf who put in a door,
That stopped the spider who started to crawl,
That shocked the mummy who raised the wall,
Inside the house that monsters built.

This is the skeleton who nailed down the floor,
That upset the werewolf who put in a door,
That stopped the spider who started to crawl,
That shocked the mummy who raised the wall,
Inside the house that monsters built.

This is Frankie who brought in a chair,
That rattled the skeleton who nailed down the floor,
That upset the werewolf who put in a door,
That stopped the spider who started to crawl,
That shocked the mummy who raised the wall,
Inside the house that monsters built.

This is the black cat who jumped in the air,
That terrified Frankie who brought in a chair,
That rattled the skeleton who nailed down the floor,
That upset the werewolf who put in a door,

That stopped the spider who started to crawl,
That shocked the mummy who raised the wall,
Inside the house that monsters built.

These are the bats who hung from a beam,
That scared the black cat who jumped in the air,
That terrified Frankie who brought in a chair,
That rattled the skeleton who nailed down the floor,
That upset the werewolf who put in a door,

That stopped the spider who started to crawl,
That shocked the mummy who raised the wall,
Inside the house that monsters built.

This is the zombie who let out a scream,
That scattered the bats who hung from a beam,
That scared the black cat who jumped in the air,
That terrified Frankie who brought in a chair,
hat rattled the skeleton who nailed down the floor,
That upset the werewolf who put in a door,
That stopped the spider who started to crawl,
That shocked the mummy who raised the wall,
Inside the house that monsters built.

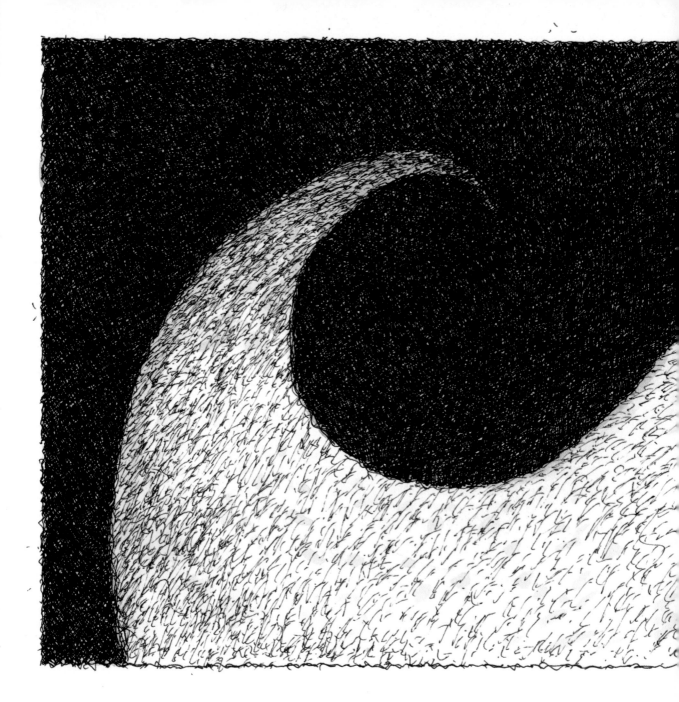

This is the ghost who shouted out, "Boo!"
That startled the zombie who let out a scream,
That scattered the bats who hung from a beam,
That scared the black cat who jumped in the air,
That terrified Frankie who brought in a chair,

That rattled the skeleton who nailed down the floor,
That upset the werewolf who put in a door,
That stopped the spider who started to crawl,
That shocked the mummy who raised the wall,
Inside the house that monsters built.

This is the old witch who stirred up the brew,
That spooked the ghost who shouted out, "Boo!"
That startled the zombie who let out a scream,
That scattered the bats who hung from a beam,
That scared the black cat who jumped in the air,
That terrified Frankie who brought in a chair,
That rattled the skeleton who nailed down the floor,
That upset the werewolf who put in a door,
That stopped the spider who started to crawl,
That shocked the mummy who raised the wall,
Inside the house that monsters built.

This is the vampire who tripped on his feet,
That stunned the old witch who stirred up the brew,
That spooked the ghost who shouted out, "Boo!"
That startled the zombie who let out a scream,
That scattered the bats who hung from a beam,
That scared the black cat who jumped in the air,
That terrified Frankie who brought in a chair,

That rattled the skeleton who nailed down the floor,
That upset the werewolf who put in a door,
That stopped the spider who started to crawl,
That shocked the mummy who raised the wall,
Inside the house that monsters built.

These are the kids who yelled, "Trick or treat!"
That woke up the vampire who tripped on his feet,

That stunned the old witch who stirred up the brew,

That spooked the ghost who shouted out, "Boo!"

That startled the zombie who let out a scream,

That scattered the bats who hung from a beam,

That scared the black cat who jumped in the air,

That terrified Frankie who brought in a chair,

That rattled the skeleton who nailed down the floor,

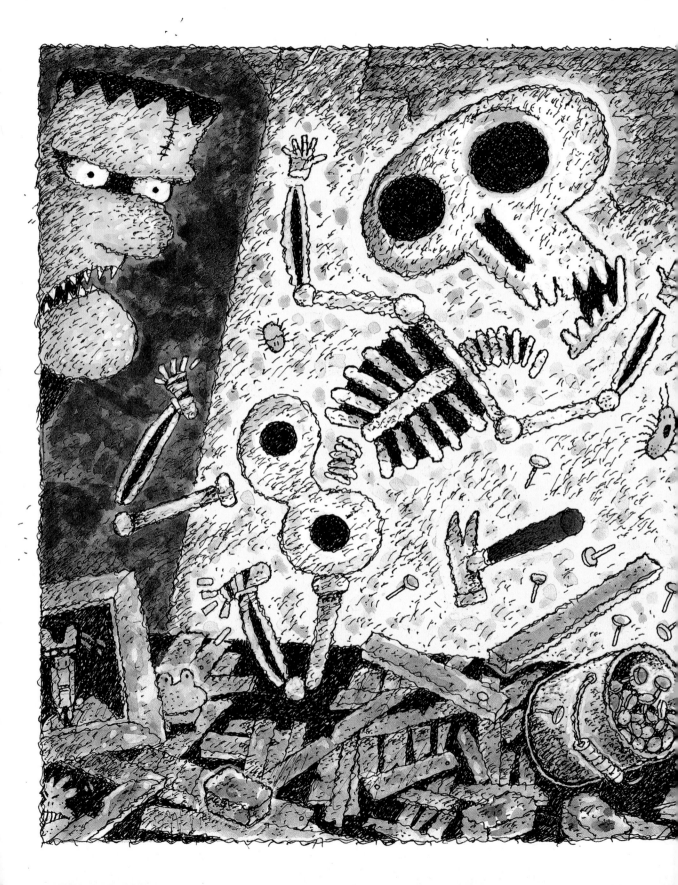

That upset the werewolf who put in a door,

That stopped the spider who started to crawl,

That shocked the mummy who raised the wall,